THE
Shaggy
DOG

Adapted by Elizabeth L. Griffen from the
Walt Disney Production

Screenplay by Bill Walsh and Lillie Hayward

SCHOLASTIC INC.
New York Toronto London Auckland Sydney Tokyo

The characters in this book were played in the motion picture, *The Shaggy Dog*, by:

MR. DANIELS	Fred MacMurray
MRS. DANIELS	Jean Hagen
WILBY	Tommy Kirk
BUZZ	Tim Considine
MOOCHIE	Kevin Corcoran
PROFESSOR PLUMCOTT	Cecil Kellaway
FRANCESCA	Roberta Shore
DR. ANDRASSY	Alexander Scourby
STEPHANO	Jacques Aubuchon
THE SPY	Strother Martin
OFFICER HANSON	James Westerfield
HANSON'S COMPANION	Forrest Lewis

The edition containing the full text of Felix Salten's THE HOUND OF FLORENCE, which suggested the screenplay for THE SHAGGY DOG, is published by Simon & Schuster, New York.

Photos copyright Walt Disney Productions

ISBN 0-590-02401-9

Copyright © 1967 Walt Disney Productions. All rights reserved. This edition is published by Scholastic Inc., by arrangement with Walt Disney Productions.

22 21 20 19 18 17 16 15 14 13 12   4 5 6 7 8/8

Printed in the U.S.A.   11

Contents

This room temporarily
closed to the public

NEXT EXHIBIT
"THE AGE OF SORCERY"

Blast-off!

IT WAS ON A SUMMER MORNING in the quiet little town of Springfield that the whole thing began. Wilby never thought so much could happen in one day. But it did.

It started like any ordinary day. The bright June air smelled sweetly of flowers, and of the sea close by. Most of the townspeople were up, but hardly anyone was out yet on the quiet tree-lined streets.

In the Daniels house, Wilby and his little brother Moochie were already busy in their workshop down in the basement; upstairs, their parents were still at the breakfast table. Mr. Daniels was reading the morning newspaper. Everything seemed peaceful.

Then: "Blast it!" exploded Mr. Daniels, slapping his paper on the table.

"What is it, dear?" asked Mrs. Daniels mildly. "A dog?"

"Right! A blasted dog! Just look at that picture! Did you ever see anything so ridiculous?" Mr. Daniels handed his wife the paper, pointing to a photograph of a handsome police dog.

"Why, he has a medal hanging around his neck," she said. "He's been decorated for bravery!"

"It's a lot of nonsense," replied her husband. "Sickly sentimentality! Giving a medal to a dog! Ugh!"

"Don't get the paper in the butter, dear," said Mrs. Daniels. "You must remember that most people *like* dogs."

"Oh? I suppose I'm some kind of freak because I don't?"

"It's nothing to be ashamed of, Wilson. Lots of other mailmen don't like dogs either. But it's not the dogs' fault. Frankly, I think dogs don't like mailmen because — well, sometimes mailmen bring bad news. Animals sense those things, you know."

"Bosh! It's because they just naturally yap and snap at a man's heels. Who in his right mind would want to own a *dog?*"

"Moochie would," said his wife, with a touch of indignation. "That boy needs a dog of his own."

"Now, let's not bring *that* up again. As long as I'm so allergic to dogs, it's out of the question." And unconsciously Mr. Daniels began to scratch his neck under the edge of his collar. "Say, where *are* the boys anyway?"

"They had breakfast early. They're down in the cellar tinkering with something."

"Tinkering? What with?"

"Something called a 'missile interceptor,'" said their mother.

"Wilby had better be tinkering with the lawn mower. If that lawn doesn't get mowed today —" A belated thought struck Mr. Daniels: "MISSILE INTERCEPTOR!"

At that moment, a low ominous rumble filled the air. The dining room began to vibrate slightly. Mr. Daniels stared in fascination as his cup and saucer danced lightly away from him across the table.

Springing to his feet, he rushed to the basement door.

"Stop that this minute!" he roared.

Down in the basement, smoke was seeping from a long rocketlike projectile fastened into the bed of an old coaster wagon. The projectile, on its mobile launching pad, rumbled and shuddered from time to time.

Wilby and Moochie were bent over the contraption, trying to make adjustments in a black box attached to the rocket by a mass of complicated wiring.

"Maybe you'd better switch it off," suggested Moochie worriedly.

"How can I?" retorted Wilby. "I haven't turned it *on* yet. Help me find that loose wire! Maybe it's hanging down somewhere . . ."

"There!" pointed Moochie.

Wilby worked feverishly for a few seconds. The shuddering and rumbling stopped. He took a deep breath. Sweat was pouring from his face. He lifted his eyes to find his father standing over him, a look of tightly controlled fury on his face.

"Do you realize what you almost did?"

"Yes sir," said Wilby weakly.

"I figure we'd better move it to the vacant lot next time," said Moochie nervously.

His father eyed him fiercely.

"There will be no next time! Dismantle that thing. Take it apart, nut from bolt, and never — I repeat, NEVER — build anything like it within a hundred miles of this spot!"

Beauty and the Beast

MOOCHIE AND WILBY WERE SITTING on the front steps with their friend Buzz, whose battered bright-yellow sports car was parked at the curb.

"Our whole summer's ruined," Wilby was saying. "You don't know what plans we had for that rocket!"

"I know you got off a lot easier than I would've," answered Buzz. "If *I'd* almost blown up the house . . . boy!" Buzz stopped, remembering how enthusiastic he'd been about the rocket, and added comfortingly, "We can probably think of something to invent — something else just as good, like a racing car — can't you, Wilby?"

"Nothing could possibly be half as good," said Wilby.

"Unless," said Moochie, "it was a *dog*. Even Wilby can't make a dog — and if he could, we couldn't keep it."

His words hung mournfully in the air. The boys saw their whole summer slowly collapsing like a punctured balloon.

Suddenly they heard music, or rather a musical auto horn that played a military tune. Then, at the end of the street, appeared a strange procession — a black Ferrari, followed by a huge moving van. As the car came closer, the boys could make out three figures in the front seat: a man at the wheel, a large shaggy dog hanging out the other side, and in between them a very pretty girl. The boys stared — Moochie at the dog, Buzz at the girl, and Wilby at all three.

As the car went past, the girl gave them a dazzling smile. She was not just pretty, she was beautiful. Then the car turned into the driveway of the large house across the street.

Moochie could stand it no longer. He tore into the house, letting the screen door slam behind him.

"Mom! Pop! Look what's moving in across the street!"

His parents were already at the window.

"You mean *who,* dear. *Who's* moving in," said his mother. Then she exclaimed, "Why, it must be the new curator for the county museum. I heard that he'd rented that house, but I didn't know he was coming so soon. Won't it be nice to see lights again in that gloomy old Coverly house!"

"Who's the girl?" asked Mr. Daniels.

"His daughter, perhaps, or a niece," replied his wife. "My! She's pretty, isn't she?"

"Wait a minute," snorted Mr. Daniels. "What's that thing? How dare they bring a camel into this neighborhood? Oh no!" he choked. "It's a *dog!* A blasted, dratted dog!" His voice weakened. "I'll have to move into the back bedroom."

"Now don't go all to pieces, Wilson," said Mrs. Daniels. "You know that dog thing is all in your mind."

"Oh sure! I itch. My sinuses are swelling up. My throat is getting that chokey feeling. Those old Pekingese wounds in my ankle are throbbing like bongo drums. And it's all in my mind!" Mr. Daniels left the room indignantly, breathing heavily and clawing at his collar.

Outside, the shaggy dog had leaped down from the car, followed more sedately by his beautiful mistress. She was fully aware that she was the center of attention of the boys across the street. She stopped to fondle the big dog, murmuring sweet nothings to him, but loud enough for the boys to hear.

Wilby and Buzz were struck dumb by her loveliness and sophistication. Was it *French* that she was speaking to her dog? They caught a *n'est-ce pas.* But before they could recover, she had disappeared into the house. The dog nosed around the yard awhile, then came trotting across the street to Wilby.

"What do you know? He likes me!" exclaimed Wilby, pleased and surprised.

The dog certainly *did* like Wilby. He licked the boy's face and wagged his tail, as if he were greeting an old friend. Unfortunately, he ignored Moochie, who came dashing out to pet him, and Buzz. Wilby was both flattered and puzzled. But Buzz was not impressed.

"So he likes you — that's *his* problem," he observed.

11

"I'm more interested in the little ma'mselle who owns him. I'd better take him back to her. She'll probably be worried. Come on, pooch."

"Just a minute, Buzz," interrupted Wilby. "This dog came to *me*. We'll *both* take him back."

They crossed the street to the old mansion, mounted the steps, and rang the bell. A butler opened the door. Unsmiling, he regarded the boys.

"Yes?" he asked coldly.

"Uh," began Wilby, "we've brought your dog back."

"The ma'mselle's dog," added Buzz quickly.

At this moment the girl appeared in the door. How beautiful she was! Her dark hair gleamed, and her smile was radiant.

Buzz stepped forward.

"Uh — we thought you'd be worried about your dog. So we brought him back."

"How *good* of you!" she said. "My name is Francesca, and this" — laying her hand on the dog's head — "is Chiffon."

"I'm Buzz Miller," said Buzz. "I own the car parked over there, and this is Wilby Daniels. He lives right across the street."

"Why, then we're neighbors," said Francesca, smiling. "Won't you come in?"

The three entered the house, the shaggy dog following. Inside it was cool, and suddenly darker than the bright outdoors. The living room was large, and already partly furnished — the butler had seen to that. From time to time moving men passed through, carrying large crates. Wilby tried to guess what was in them; then he heard the butler say, "Lean the paintings against this wall, and put the statues over there."

"Her father's a collector," Wilby thought. "He collects art."

"I'm afraid you'll have to excuse the looks of the house," said Francesca. "We're just moving in, you know."

"Great Pete," said Buzz, looking around, "Look at all the stuff!"

Francesca smiled.

"Some of it is 'stuff,' as you say. But some of it is rather priceless. My uncle is a collector." Wilby nodded. The girl paused before a large picture that had been uncrated and was leaning against the wall.

Buzz and Wilby stood staring at it. Chiffon pushed in between them and crowded Wilby against a nearby sofa. Wilby sat down abruptly, and the dog tried to climb into his lap.

"Well, look at that!" said Francesca. "I've never seen Chiffon take such a fancy to anyone before."

"Sure is friendly," came Wilby's muffled voice from under the dog.

Buzz felt it was up to him to get the conversation back on the track.

"Say," he said brightly, "you really go for this art bit, don't you?"

"I know a little about it," said Francesca. "I work with my uncle."

"Who's *that?*" asked Buzz, pointing to the painting in front of them. It showed a woman in a long velvet dress with a large shaggy dog at her feet. Her rich clothing and the furnishings in the background seemed to be from another time and place.

14

"She was one of the Borgias," replied Francesca. "You've heard about them, of course?"

"Oh yeah. Sure," said Buzz uncertainly.

"Long ago in Italy, they were notorious for their evil deeds," went on Francesca. "Poison and things like that, you know. Some people thought the Borgias even dabbled in black magic."

Wilby was frowning at the painting.

"Say, that dog in the picture there . . . Isn't he the same kind as yours?"

"Yes," said Francesca, "a Bratislavian sheep dog. The breed has mostly died out now. Chiffon is one of the few left."

The man whom they had seen driving the car earlier now entered the room. He was carrying a package.

"Excuse me, Francesca. Would you be good enough to take these Orsini artifacts to the museum? Dr. Howard is waiting for them."

"Certainly, Uncle Mikhail," replied Francesca. Turning to the boys, she said, "This is my uncle, Dr. Andrassy."

"How do you do, gentlemen," said Dr. Andrassy. "If you'll excuse me . . ." he added, as two moving men approached.

"Hey," said Buzz, "How's about me driving you to the museum? I've got my car outside."

"Yes," said Wilby quickly. "We'll *both* take you."

Francesca accepted, and the three of them piled into Buzz's sports car. Summer was back on the right track again — or so it seemed.

The Age of Sorcery

"WHAT A SWEET LITTLE MUSEUM," said Francesca, as they pulled up in front of the town's modest museum.

"Not bad," replied Buzz. "I spend a lot of time around this place. Studying the arts."

"Then how come you got lost getting here?" asked Wilby.

Buzz ignored the question. He led Francesca into the museum.

"Here's something you'd like," he said, pointing to a statue. "Not bad-looking, is it?"

"*C'est charmant,*" murmured Francesca.

"Personally, I go more for the old fossils," said Wilby, walking past the statue.

As soon as Wilby's back was turned, Buzz took Francesca's arm and steered her through one of the archways.

"Francesca," continued Wilby, "get this . . ." He turned and saw that he was alone. "Francesca! Buzz! Where the heck are they?"

Annoyed, he looked through another archway and noticed a door marked "Renaissance Room." The door was ajar. He stepped inside.

Eerie shadows filled the dimly lighted room. As his eyes became used to the darkness, Wilby could make out strange figures. All of them seemed to be engaged in dark deeds of violence.

"Wax figures," thought Wilby after his first surprise. In the showcases he could see instruments of torture, poison-potion cups, and daggers.

A small sign on a stand near the door read: "This room temporarily closed to the public. Next exhibit — The Age of Sorcery." Wilby did not see the sign.

"Buzz . . . ?" he called.

Across the room, a figure in a black flowing cloak seemed to move. Wilby turned to go, then turned back. The figure *was* moving. It raised an arm menacingly. Wilby was intrigued. As he approached the figure, a low moan issued from it. Wilby froze in his tracks. But at the sound of a chuckle, he began to breathe again.

From behind the black cloak of the figure stepped a plump, smiling, elderly gentleman.

"Gosh, you scared me, Professor," gasped Wilby.

"Serves you right," said the white-haired man, his eyes twinkling. "You shouldn't be wandering around in here before the exhibit's open."

"Sorry, Professor Plumcott," said Wilby. "I was looking for my friends."

18

"Well, you've stumbled into the delightfully evil days of the Borgias here."

"Yeah. Well, I better be . . ." began Wilby, eager to get away.

"Wilby, do you realize that people in those days used sorcery, black magic, witchcraft, shape-shifting? They even knew how to cast spells."

"What's shape-shifting?" asked Wilby.

Professor Plumcott lifted a tray of jewelry — old necklaces, rings, brooches, and bracelets — from a showcase. It was clear that his work had to go on, even during a discussion of one of his favorite subjects.

"A most interesting practice — shape-shifting. It's the medieval art of borrowing someone else's body to live in for a while. You've read of humans being turned into foxes, cats, and other creatures, haven't you?"

19

"Gosh, Professor," said Wilby, "you don't believe in that stuff, do you?"

"Wilby, today people laugh at those things. But don't we have to admit honestly that there are times . . . dark, lonely nights . . . when something stirs inside us — a reawakening of ancient fears and feelings?"

"You mean superstition?" Wilby asked scornfully.

"Some call it that," replied the professor. "But, on the other hand, couldn't it be some instinct buried deep in the human heart — something telling us that such things as black magic and shape-shifting do exist, because they really happened?"

Wilby felt uneasy.

"So how come people don't know about them today?" he asked.

"Who can tell?" murmured the professor. "Each new age gains a little knowledge; each loses a little."

"Well, I have to be going now, Professor," said Wilby hastily. "Got to find my friends."

"Yes, yes, of course," said the professor. "Run along. But drop in and see me again sometime, Wilby. In the meantime — oh, *look out!*"

Wilby had bumped into a table and upset the tray of jewelry. Both he and the professor grabbed at it. They caught the tray, but not before some of the pieces had fallen to the floor. Wilby went down on his knees to pick them up, this time banging against a showcase of Venetian glass.

The professor looked alarmed.

"Wilby, why don't you run along?" he said firmly. "I'll take care of these."

20

"Sure it's all right?" asked Wilby. "I'm awfully sorry."

"Quite all right," answered the professor. He watched anxiously as Wilby made his way to the door.

"See you," Wilby called. He turned and waved at the professor as he stumbled out of the room.

The professor breathed a sigh of relief. Then, his good humor restored, he turned cheerfully back to his witches and poisoners, and the other waxen villains.

Wilby had to walk home. He reached his street just in time to see Buzz drive away from Francesca's house. As Buzz passed him, Wilby shook his fist. Buzz laughed, honked several times, and roared past.

How to Be
a Shape-shifter

THAT EVENING AFTER DINNER, Moochie and Wilby
were down in their basement workshop examining what
was left of the morning's disaster. The workshop held
an interesting collection. Along one wall was an old sink
with a counter full of chemical equipment. Another wall
held shelves full of labeled boxes. In the middle of the
floor stood a tool bench. On an old table to one side were
cages of mice and hamsters. A large turtle ambled across
the floor. In the farthest corner was the coaster wagon,
holding the remains of the dismantled rocket.

"There," said Wilby nodding toward it, "lies the interceptor that got intercepted."

"By Pop," added Moochie. His face brightened. "So
now we can look for fossils over at the quarry. How
about it, Wilby? Let's go first thing in the morning!"

Wilby was sorting through a box of electrical wire.

"We can't go anywhere till we get this place cleaned up. You heard Pop."

"Let's finish it up tonight then," said Moochie. "We can do it!" And he began energetically picking up stray equipment.

Two hours later the workshop actually looked neat.

"First time it's been really clean since Thanksgiving," said Wilby.

Just then they heard the door open at the top of the cellar stairs. It was their father.

"All right, boys," he said. "Time for bed."

"Be right up, Pop," said Moochie. "Coming, Wilby?"

Wilby was on his knees, searching among some bottles under the chemistry counter.

"In a minute," he answered, as Moochie went up the stairs. Wilby started to get up, then stopped short. Slowly he reached down and, from the cuff of his trousers, picked up something he saw gleaming there.

It was a ring — a gold ring, strangely carved. Wilby stared at it, puzzled.

"What's this?" he said out loud. He turned it over and over. To himself he thought, "Now, how do you suppose — oh, I know. I'll bet it's the Professor's. When I spilled that tray of jewelry some of it fell, and this ring must have caught in my pants cuff."

Wilby's voice trailed off as he examined the ring, fascinated. Then he saw that what had looked like a carved design was really letters and words. Strange words. One by one he spelled them out:

IN CANIS CORPORE TRANSMUTO

"It's Latin," he thought. "Wish I knew more than just first-year Latin. *Canis* — I think that means 'dog.' — 'Into dog' . . . something — 'corpse' or 'body'? . . . *transmuto* . . . 'change' . . ."

Wilby slipped the ring on his forefinger and held it out to admire. The Latin phrase kept jingling in his brain. Unconsciously he put a beat to it.

"IN canis CORpore TRANSmuto!" *he said out loud.*
There was a sudden hush in the air. The small animals in their cages fled to the farthest corners. A patch of fur appeared on Wilby's hand.

Wilby stared at his hand, as it grew more and more stubby — like a dog's paw! Then he became aware of thick hair hanging down over his eyes. He rushed to a mirror on the wall and peered into it. A large shaggy face peered back at him. A vaguely familiar face.

"Great Christmas! What's happened? That's Francesca's dog — but it's me!" squawked Wilby hoarsely. "But it can't be!" Wilby groaned. "That ring! Good grief, I'm a shape-shifter! A dog — Pop — ooh," Wilby's groan sounded strangely like a dog's whine.

Upstairs, Mr. Daniels was turning out the lights before going to bed. He paused, glanced irritably at his watch, and frowned. "What's keeping that boy?" he muttered. He strode to the basement door, flung it open, and peered down.

"Wilby? *Wilby!* Come on now. It's getting late."

In the basement, a large shaggy dog scrambled wildly behind a large carton.

"Okay, Pop," it said hoarsely, in Wilby's voice.

"Are you catching cold, Wilby?" asked his father. "I thought your mother told you to wear a sweater down there."

"I *got* a sweater."

"*Have* a sweater. Anyway it's time to come up now, so let's get a move on." His father went into the kitchen for a bedtime snack, leaving the basement door ajar behind him.

Across the street, in the living room of the Coverly mansion, Francesca sat reading on the large sofa. Without taking her eyes off the book she held, she reached out as if to stroke something beside her. Her hand touched — empty air. She looked at the vacant place where a few minutes ago her shaggy dog had lain, in surprise.

"Why, where's Chiffon? He was here just a second ago!" She looked at the rug; then, rather wildly, around the room. "Has that dog run off again? He's been acting very strange lately. Well, it's a new house. It will take him a little while to get used to it, I suppose. Still . . ." She returned to her book, wearing a frown of displeasure.

Back in the Daniels' basement, Wilby, his shape now fully shifted into a large shaggy dog, sat dejectedly. Suddenly his head snapped up.

"Professor Plumcott!" said Wilby's voice. "*He* can help me!" The dog started for the stairs, and stopped. "Pop!" he whispered. Then he went up, cautiously.

A black nose appeared at the basement door, then

a shaggy muzzle. Mr. Daniels was moving about in the kitchen. The dog dashed across the floor, stopped at the front screen door, and nudged it open. Slipping through, Wilby let the door shut gently against his dog shape, and then galloped off wildly into the night, in the direction of the museum.

A Midnight Visit

IT WAS NEARLY MIDNIGHT, but in the back windows of the museum a few lights still burned dimly. At the back door the janitor, mop and bucket in hand, was just going inside. As he walked into the building, a shaggy dog slipped out of the nearby bushes and slid silently in behind him. The dog waited near the back door until the janitor was busy at the sink of the wash closet. Then he padded softly down the shadowy corridor in the direction of the Renaissance Room.

The door of the Renaissance Room stood ajar. Inside, it was dimly lit by the reddish light of an antique lamp. Wilby-the-dog looked in cautiously; he was relieved to see only Professor Plumcott. In his shirt-sleeves, the professor was still happily at work among his treasures. Just at this moment he was adjusting a jeweled headdress on the wax figure of one of the Borgia princes.

"Professor Plumcott?" said Wilby-the-dog in his hoarse voice.

"Yes," replied the Professor absently. He turned and saw the dog sitting nearby. "Hello, fella." He patted the dog and then went back to work.

"Professor," repeated Wilby. "I've got to talk to you."

The professor looked mildly reproachful. "Now you know dogs aren't allowed in here."

"But I'm *not* a dog — not really. I'm Wilby Daniels."

Professor Plumcott turned around at this. He looked interested.

"Wilby Daniels? Are you really?" He smiled delightedly. "Well, well. I'm not at all surprised. First time I saw you, I said to myself, 'That boy has the makings of a shape-shifter.'"

"You did?" asked Wilby.

"Of course. There's nothing so very unusual about shape-shifting. It's quite common — that is, it *used* to be, back in the fifteenth century. How did you manage it?"

"I think this ring had something to do with it," said Wilby, holding out his paw.

The professor looked more delighted than ever.

"The Borgia ring! Where did you get it? I've been looking all over for it." Carefully he removed the ring from the dog's toe.

"It must've fallen into the cuff of my trousers," said Wilby. "And when I read those words on it . . ."

"A very rare and unusual ring," the professor went on, heedless of Wilby's story. "Thank you for returning it." He carried the ring lovingly to the jewel cabinet.

"Hey, wait a minute!" cried Wilby in dismay.

"Eh?" said the professor. "What's the matter?"

Wilby waved a paw helplessly. "How about *me?*"

"Well, what about you?" asked Professor Plumcott. He looked quite puzzled.

"I don't want to be a dog!"

"You don't?"

"Of course not!" said Wilby. Anyway, I can't — even if I wanted to, which I don't. Pop won't *have* a dog in the house. Can't you help me?"

The professor looked thoughtful.

"Wilby, I think that you've got yourself involved with some old spell that was laid on this ring — probably by one of the Borgias. Sounds just like them."

"But how do I get out of it?"

"Good heavens, boy," said Professor Plumcott, "how do I know? There are all kinds of spells. Some break themselves after a while. Some just come and go like a headache."

"Come and go?" asked Wilby fearfully.

The professor nodded.

"Sometimes you might be a dog for several hours, and sometimes a boy — sometimes longer, sometimes shorter. Who knows? That's what makes it interesting."

"But, Professor," insisted Wilby, "what can I do to break this spell?"

"Well, the usual thing in the old days was to hire a professional sorcerer."

"*Sorcerer?*" squeaked Wilby. "Where can I find a sorcerer?"

"Oh, I don't suppose there are any sorcerers around today."

Wilby was becoming desperate.

"Professor, you've just *got* to help me!"

"Now, Wilby, don't get all excited. That's the worst thing you can do. Keep calm. Avoid excitement. Maybe the spell will wear itself out. In any case," he added cheerfully, "you'll wind up as one or the other — a boy or a dog."

"Which one?" asked Wilby uneasily.

"What difference does it make?"

"It makes a lot of difference! I told you — I don't want to be a dog!"

"Yes, yes, you did say that." The professor appeared to be in deep thought. At last he said, "An act of heroism might break the spell."

Wilby pricked up his ears.

"What kind of heroism?"

"You remember *The Hound of Florence*, of course?" asked the professor.

"No sir," said Wilby, scratching his neck with his hindleg. (Fleas were no joke, he'd already decided.)

"Quite a famous story," went on the professor, enthusiastically. "A young man changed into a dog — same as you did. Then one night he got into a fight heroically defending a girl from the attentions of an evil duke." Here the professor seized a wicked-looking dagger from a nearby case, grabbed Wilby by the collar, and seemed about to plunge the dagger into him. Wilby struggled vainly. "The duke plunged his dagger into the dog! The dog fell to the ground . . ." The professor dropped Wilby. "Then, as the poor animal lay there with the dagger in his heart, he changed back into a man."

Wilby looked up, horrified.

"You mean I've got to have a dagger stuck in my heart? But that would kill me!"

"Wilby," said Professor Plumcott irritably, "you've missed the whole point of the story. I only tried to show you that it's possible to break such a spell. Now if you'll excuse me, I'm quite busy."

Wilby slowly got to his feet, head and tail sunk in dejection. "I'm sorry to have bothered you, Professor."

"Quite all right," said the professor, softening. "Tell you what, Wilby. I'll write to a friend of mine. He's an expert on these ancient spells. Perhaps he can help you."

"I'd sure appreciate that," said Wilby.

"Of course," continued the professor, "the letter may take awhile to reach him. He's on an expedition in Africa."

"Isn't there anything I can do in the meantime?" asked Wilby desperately.

"Yes," said the professor cheerfully. "Be happy. Keep a stiff upper lip."

"Thanks," said Wilby. With head sunk still lower, the unhappy shape-shifter padded out.

Moonlight slanted across the boys' bedroom, where Moochie had been asleep for several hours. The sound of the bedroom door slamming shut wakened him suddenly. He opened his eyes, but still seemed to be dreaming. By the dresser stood a beautiful shaggy dog — with Wilby's pajamas in his mouth. Moochie closed his eyes. When he opened them again a little later, he could still see the dog. It was now wearing the pajamas and climbing into Wilby's bed. Moochie smiled and drifted blissfully back to sleep.

Moochie's New Dog

MORNING DAWNED BRIGHTLY. Sunlight had replaced moonlight in the boys' bedroom when Moochie opened his eyes. A sharp rap on the door brought him, yawning, to a sitting position.

"Wilby! Moochie! Time to get up," came their father's voice.

"Be right with you, Pop," said Moochie. Suddenly he stopped yawning and looked excitedly over at his brother's bed. "Hey, Wilby, I had the funniest dream last night!" He hopped out of bed and sat down beside the large lump under Wilby's blanket. "I dreamed you were a dog!" He gave the lump a poke. "Come on, Wilby. Wake up!"

The lump stirred.

"It was the greatest dream," went on Moochie. "You

came into the room as a big old shaggy dog, and . . . hey, Wilby, listen!" He stripped back the covers.

Pure, radiant joy lighted Moochie's face.

"Oh *boy!* How did *you* get in here?"

"What do you mean — how did I get in here?" said the dog grumpily. "I live here."

Moochie's eyes widened.

"You talk just like Wilby!"

"I *am* Wilby!"

"No . . . you're a dog!"

"Huh?" Wilby leaped out of bed and ran to the mirror over the dresser. With his front paws on the dresser, he stared into the mirror. It was true then — still the same. He hadn't changed back in the night, as he had hoped. Suppose he *never* changed back! But to Moochie he said only, "Gosh . . . I *am* a dog!"

Moochie was beside himself with joy.

"Do you think Pop'll let me keep you? I'll be good to you, Wilby — honest I will! I'll buy you a license and get you a basket to sleep in and — boy! We'll have great times together!" A sudden cloud crossed his face, "Oh-oh . . ."

"What's the matter?" asked Wilby.

"I hope Pop won't shoot you! You know he swore the first time he caught a dog in the house, he'd . . ."

"You two better be up when I open that door," said their father.

There was a wild scramble as Wilby looked for a place to hide. Desperately he jumped back into bed, and Moochie hauled the covers up over him. A split second later, Mr. Daniels loomed in the doorway.

"Come on, you birds. Let's get with it. *Wilby!*" Outraged by the figure still in bed, he started toward it.

In a frenzy of activity to block the way, Moochie grabbed his harmonica from the dresser.

"Hey, Pop, listen to this!" Moochie started to play very loudly something that sounded like "Pop Goes the Weasel."

"What's the matter with you?" asked his father, slowing down.

"I just learned it. Listen!"

"Now cut out the nonsense and get dressed." Mr. Daniels reached over and gave the hidden dog a tremendous whack on the rear. As he left the room, Mr. Daniels was beginning to scratch.

After a moment, Wilby peered out from under the covers. Then he sat up.

"Why oh why did this have to happen to me?"

But Moochie was all enthusiasm again.

"Oh, Wilby," he exclaimed, "it's just *terrific!* Tell me what happened. Here, let me help you . . ." And he began helping Wilby out of his pajamas.

"Well, I don't know exactly what happened," replied Wilby. "You remember when we were down in the basement last night . . ." And he told Moochie the whole story.

"But did Professor Plumcott say you'd have to stay a dog all your life?" asked Moochie.

"He doesn't know exactly."

"Gee, I hope you will!" said Moochie fervently. "I mean, as long as I can't have a dog any other way . . ."

"Well, *I'm* not going to be your dog, so get that out of your head!"

"Oh, Wilby, I'll teach you all kinds of tricks. You

know, like rolling over and begging, and all that stuff. I'll bet even Pop'll learn to love you!"

"*Boys!*" The command came from downstairs, from the dining room.

"You better stay here," said Moochie hurriedly. "I'll tell them you're not hungry."

"*Not hungry!* I'm starved!"

"I'll sneak something up later. You like bones? Nice meaty bones?"

"You know what I like," said Wilby angrily. "Bacon and eggs and toast with marmalade and peanut butter on it! Hurry up!"

"Don't worry, boy," said Moochie gently. "I'm going to take good care of you!"

Wilby snarled, and Moochie left hastily.

Downstairs at the breakfast table, the first thing that Mr. Daniels had said was, "Frieda, have you seen any dogs around here?"

His wife looked surprised.

"Of course not. They wouldn't dare come into our yard!"

Mr. Daniels picked up the morning paper, blinked a few times, and again turned to his wife.

"Are my eyes getting puffy?"

"Well, your eyes have always been a *little* puffy, dear," she replied.

"Oh, I know," said her husband irritably, "but they feel as though they're swelling shut. If I thought for a moment . . ." He peered under the table. Then he got up, crossed to the window, and looked out. No dog in sight. He sat down at the table again and looked accusingly at his wife. "You're always telling me how Moochie wants a dog. I know you two wouldn't gang up on me. Or would you?"

"Of course not. Wilson, do sit down and eat your eggs before they get cold."

Just then Moochie came tearing down the stairs, sat down, and began to talk and eat rapidly, glancing nervously over at the stairs every few minutes. But Wilby-the-dog crept down unnoticed by his parents and went into the kitchen. He hid behind the kitchen door while Mrs. Daniels filled a platter with bacon and carried it into the dining room. When she came back into the kitchen, she saw a dog just reaching for the toast.

"Oh-oh! How did you get in? Out! Quick! Out!" But the dog turned such hungry, pleading eyes upward

that she gave in. "All right. Here," she said, holding out a piece of toast to him.

"Frieda! Where's my toast?" from the dining room.

Mrs. Daniels hurriedly picked up the plate of toast and carried it into the dining room. Behind her the door was swinging back and forth. Each swing revealed the dog.

Mr. Daniels started, leaning far out from his chair for a better view.

"Frieda," he said quietly. "Is there a dog in the kitchen?"

"Dog? What kind of a dog?" she asked guiltily.

"That's all I wanted to know," said Mr. Daniels, getting up. He had a grim expression on his face.

"Pop," cried Moochie. "Where are you going?"

"To the hall closet."

"What for?"

"For my gun!"

"But, Pop," Moochie protested, grabbing his father's arm, "you can't shoot your own —"

"My own *what?*"

"Your — own neighbor's dog!"

"Oh, *can't* I!"

Moochie raised his voice frantically: "POP! Don't shoot that poor dog!"

At last Wilby heard. He dropped on all fours and hurtled through the back door to the yard.

A second later Mr. Daniels burst into the kitchen, his shotgun on the ready.

Wilby scooted under the clothesline and plunged into the bushes.

Mr. Daniels rushed from the house a moment too late.

"Run, you cowardly fleabag!" he shouted. "If I ever catch you on my property again . . ."

But Wilby was safe. He had arrived, panting, at the kitchen door of the Coverly mansion. His nose told him that breakfast was in progress.

Wilby-the-dog, looking exactly like Chiffon, scratched on the door.

Undercover at Coverly

THE BUTLER WAS BUSY at the big old-fashioned stove in the Coverly kitchen. He was getting breakfast ready for Francesca, who stood in the doorway of the breakfast room, discussing Chiffon's strange behavior with him.

"I just don't understand it, do you, Stephano? He's never stayed away all night before."

"I'm sure, mademoiselle," said Stephano, "that he will return for his meals."

At this moment they both heard Wilby scratching at the kitchen door. Stephano opened it and Wilby-the-dog darted in.

Francesca threw her arms around him. "Chiffon, *mon petit!* I've been so worried about you. What have you been up to?"

Wilby, embarrassed by all this warm affection, hung his head.

"Don't worry," continued Francesca. "You're forgiven. Would you like some breakfast?"

At the mention of food, Wilby leaped up and frolicked happily about the kitchen.

"Oh, you *are* hungry! Stephano!"

Wilby's joy came to an abrupt end when he saw what Stephano was doing. He was pouring dry dog food into a bowl and moistening it with milk. Wilby wrinkled up his nose in distaste. Then, because Francesca and Stephano were watching him, he tried to act like Chiffon. Stolidly he settled down and tried to chew and swallow the unappetizing stuff.

The doorbell rang, and Stephano left the room to answer it. Wilby immediately trotted over to the breakfast table. He looked beseechingly at Francesca, and then at the bacon and eggs on her plate. The girl shook her head at him, smiling.

"You rogue!" she said. But she held out a strip of bacon. Wilby swallowed it in one gulp.

Stephano, meanwhile, had opened the door to a small, hard-faced man carrying a briefcase.

"Yes?"

"Dr. Andrassy is expecting me," said the stranger. "My name is Thurm."

"Yes, Mr. Thurm. Come in." Stephano led the way up the stairs to Dr. Andrassy's study. Francesca heard the study door close. "Hmm, I wonder who that is," she mused. She fastened a dog collar on Wilby.

A few minutes later Francesca, holding Wilby by

41

the collar, opened the door of her uncle's study. She stopped when she saw the stranger, and said,

"Oh — I beg your pardon."

Dr. Andrassy looked at her coldly.

"Francesca, in the future I wish you'd be good enough to knock before you enter this study."

"I'm terribly sorry," said Francesca. She seemed surprised at her uncle's manner.

"Mr. Thurm, this is my niece, Francesca."

"How do you do," said Francesca with a smile.

Thurm bowed silently.

"What did you want, dear?" continued Andrassy, speaking this time in his usual manner.

"I'm going shopping, Uncle. I thought I'd leave Chiffon here with you, so he won't run away again." She ruffled the dog's ears and planted a kiss on his nose. (Wilby reeled dizzily.) "Forgive me for interrupting. It won't happen again." To the visitor she nodded. "Mr. Thurm . . ."

Thurm bowed slightly as she left, closing the door behind her.

"A most attractive young lady," he said.

"She's a nice child," replied Andrassy. "Now concerning that second sketch . . ." and he turned toward the drawings on the desk before them.

"Does she know the purpose of your coming here?" asked Thurm.

"Of course not."

"She suspects nothing?"

Wilby pricked up his ears. What were they talking about?

"Nothing," said Andrassy coldly. "I find the presence

of a niece useful to me at this time. Now suppose we turn our attention to your sketches, Mr. Thurm."

"Of course, Doctor. As for this second sketch . . ."

Wilby tried to look at the papers on the desk, as the two men continued to talk. Finally the dog pushed in between them and took a good look. The sketches seemed to be diagrams of some sort. Absently, Andrassy pushed the shaggy head out of the way. It came back. He pushed it away again.

"This checks, for the most part," he said, "with the data we now have. Section 32 is the key to the entire project."

Wilby, having been shoved away from the desk, stood on his hind legs, trying to see over Thurm to what Andrassy was pointing.

Thurm started to speak, stopped, and turned to stare at the dog looking over his shoulder.

"All right, Chiffon," said Andrassy. "That's enough."

Again Thurm started to speak, and again he turned to look at Wilby.

"I'm sorry, Dr. Andrassy. Does that dog have to be here?"

"Come on, Chiffon," said Andrassy firmly. He dragged Wilby to the door, opened it, and called, "Stephano!" When Stephano appeared, Andrassy said sharply, "Take him out of here. If he runs away again, I'll hold you responsible."

Andrassy returned to his study, closing the door behind him.

Stephano struggled downstairs with Wilby.

"You always cause me trouble, don't you?" he asked bitterly.

Wilby almost broke away, but Stephano tightened his grip.

"In there with you, my clever dog," he muttered, thrusting Wilby into a small room. Quickly Stephano closed the door, locked it, and put the key into his pocket. "Now let's see you get out of *there*." His footsteps moved down the hall and out of hearing.

Wilby looked around him. The room in which he found himself seemed to be a sort of storeroom. It was full of trunks, suitcases, clothes, a sewing machine, a box of tools. There was a window, but it was too high to be of any use.

Wilby circled the room twice. Then, discouraged, he lay down and tried to think what to do.

*Was he imagining things, or did his paws . . . ?
Were they . . . ? They were! They were beginning to
look like hands!*

The empty couch where Chiffon had been lying the
night before shimmered strangely in the sunlight. Suddenly Chiffon appeared. He woke up and shook himself.

Back in the storeroom, Wilby was capering about
wildly, as he unfastened the dog collar around his neck.
"Yeeeow! It's me! *Me!* Good old Wilby!" He clasped
his hands over his head in a sign of victory.

When he had overcome his excitement, the boy examined the door. Just as he hoped — the hinge plates
were on the inside. Searching through the toolbox, he
soon found a screwdriver. In short order he had pulled
the pins out of the hinge plates and carefully set the
whole door to one side. He stepped quietly out, to be
greeted by a joyful, bouncing, noisy Chiffon.

Wilby couldn't quiet the dog. At last he threw the
screwdriver down the hall, and while Chiffon was chasing it, Wilby slipped out and away.

A moment later Stephano came along with a coffee
tray. To his amazement, Chiffon came bounding toward
him. Stephano stared, unbelieving, at the unhinged door
and back at Chiffon, who proudly dropped the screwdriver at his feet.

The Country Club Dance

Wᴵʟʙʏ ꜰʟᴇᴅ ꜰʀᴏᴍ ᴛʜᴇ ɢʟᴏᴏᴍʏ Cᴏᴠᴇʀʟʏ ʜᴏᴜꜱᴇ out into the summer sunshine. He felt wonderfully light-hearted, and free for the first time since he had started shape-shifting. It was so good to look at the world again from his old familiar height!

Wilby took a roundabout way home, cutting through several back yards. Then he crossed the street non-chalantly and sauntered back to his own yard. As he rounded a corner of the Daniels house, he suddenly came upon Moochie. Wilby stopped to watch his brother, who was acting very strangely. He was crouched down, peering into the bushes and whistling softly.

"Wilby! Here, Wilby! Wilby! Here, boy!"

A grim look crossed Wilby's face. He now noticed that Moochie was carrying a dog collar and a rubber ball.

"Heeeere, Wilby!"

Moochie turned to find Wilby watching him. He looked uncertain.

"Wilby?" he asked with a quaver in his voice.

"Just what do you think you're doing?" Wilby asked.

Moochie was heartbroken.

"Oh gee . . ."

"What's the matter?" asked Wilby.

"You're not a dog any more!"

"You were going to put that collar on me, weren't you!" said Wilby accusingly.

Moochie looked down. "You don't have to get sore about it."

"Well," went on Wilby, "just forget it. I'm through with that dog stuff."

"You sure?" asked Moochie with disappointment.

Wilby stopped and blinked. "No," he admitted. Then with a look around, he asked, "Pop home?"

"He's in there cleaning his gun."

Wilby gulped and shuddered, then remembered he was really Wilby now. "He — isn't it about lunchtime?" he asked. "I didn't have a decent breakfast." He started for the house. Moochie hid the dog collar and rubber ball in the bushes and followed.

"Hello, son," said Mr. Daniels, as Wilby entered the living room. "Don't tell me you're going to honor us with your presence at lunch!"

"Yessir," said Wilby with enthusiasm. "I'm starved!"

Mrs. Daniels appeared in the door.

"Come along, everybody. Lunch is ready."

At the sight and smell of real food again, Wilby

could scarcely restrain himself. He sat down to the table with his family, feeling almost crazy with relief to be back in human shape.

"Wilson," his mother was saying, "if you don't mind, we'll have dinner early tonight. We're all going to the Country Club dance, you know."

"I know. Is my suit back from the cleaner's?"

"No, not yet. But it'll be ready in time," replied his wife. "By the way, dear, I've invited our new neighbors to go with us — Dr. Andrassy and his niece. The doctor can't go, but Francesca has accepted. I thought you'd be happy to hear that," she concluded, looking at Wilby with a smile.

Wilby gulped. Then he managed to smile back. After all, she didn't know he was a shape-shifter. And he did know Francesca pretty well now. The more he thought about it, the more he liked the idea.

By evening he had decided this was the best thing that had happened all summer. In the hallway he looked at his reflection in the full-length mirror. "Not bad," he thought. His pants were a little short, but nobody would notice that. He wished his hair were longer.

"Wilby," came his mother's voice from downstairs. "It's time for you to pick up Francesca."

"Can I come too?" asked Moochie.

"NO!" said Wilby. He strode down the stairs and out the front door.

When he rang the bell at the Coverly house, Francesca appeared almost at once. She looked lovely. Wilby was vaguely aware that she was wearing a pale blue dress with sparkly stuff all over it. Her hair was piled up on top of her head.

"It's so good of you and your family to ask me," she said as they walked to the Daniels' car together. "This is the first party I've gone to since Uncle and I left Paris."

Wilby held the car door open for her, trying not to think about the last time he had seen her. Everyone — or everyone but Wilby — chattered happily as they rode to the club. There was only one really awkward moment — when Francesca mentioned Chiffon. Wilby scrunched down in his seat. Fortunately, with a look at her husband, Mrs. Daniels changed the subject.

Lively dance music greeted them as they pulled up at the club. Groups of teen-agers, youngsters, and parents were talking and laughing together, moving constantly in and out of the ballroom, or standing on the steps outside.

The Daniels party was greeted warmly; Mrs. Daniels introduced Francesca all around, and she immediately became the center of attention.

Moochie started off in the direction of the food. "Moochie," his mother called. "Didn't you ask me for the first dance?"

Moochie stopped.

"Oh yeah," he said. "I forgot." Together, he and his mother moved off toward the dancers. Wilby and Francesca were already dancing. Mr. Daniels chatted with friends.

As the evening progressed, Wilby found it harder and harder to keep his dancing partner. Francesca was receiving constant attention from his friends, especially Buzz.

Finally Wilby caught up with her.

"Having a good time?" he asked.

Francesca smiled radiantly.

"Oh, there you are!" she said. "I was looking for you."

Wilby blushed.

"Dance?" he asked.

"Okay, folks," the band leader was saying, "we're turning down the lights. Next dance will be a Paul Revere."

Mr. and Mrs. Daniels were watching from the sidelines.

"Poor Wilby," said Mrs. Daniels. "He's just about to dance with Francesca for the first time in ages, and now everybody will be changing partners. It's a Paul Revere dance."

"Never saw Wilby enjoy a dance before," said Mr. Daniels. "Didn't know he could dance so well."

"There are a lot of things you don't know about Wilby," said his wife.

Moochie, overhearing the remark, grinned and almost choked on his sandwich. He turned his eyes quickly toward the dance floor as his parents joined the dancers, and searched for Wilby. Where *was* he, anyway? Moochie spotted him after a moment, dancing with Francesca. But why did he have to wear that sappy look on his face?

Suddenly Moochie started and stared open-mouthed at his brother. The lights were dim, but he was sure that he wasn't seeing things. No, he *wasn't*. Wilby's head was sprouting — long, shaggy, white hair!

Moochie dived in among the dancers. Squirming his way toward Wilby, he managed to reach him just as they began to change partners. Seizing Wilby, he grabbed his hand and pulled him aside.

"Moochie, don't give me any trouble," said Wilby. "I'm having too good a time."

"Wilby, you've *got* trouble!"

"Whaddya mean — trouble?"

"Wilby, look at your *paws!*"

Horror spread across Wilby's face. He rushed out the nearest door. Moochie followed close on his heels and pushed his brother into the shrubbery.

A moment before this, at the Coverly house, Chiffon had been sitting in his basket with a bone in his mouth. Suddenly, in one brief instant, Chiffon utterly disappeared. The bone hung in the air for a split second and then clattered to the floor.

Moochie stood staring at the shrubs. After a moment, a familiar shaggy head appeared. Then a dog emerged.

At this very second Francesca danced by the open door with Buzz. Glancing out, she caught sight of the shaggy dog.

"Buzz! There's Chiffon! Catch him!" she cried.

Buzz was out the door like a shot, but the dog had fled into the night.

An hour later, the telephone in the Daniels house rang. Mr. Daniels answered it.

"Hello . . . Wilby? Where *are* you? What happened to you? I suppose you went chasing after that girl's dog like all those other young idiots? What?" A pause. "Stay at Buzz's house tonight? I suppose so. All right." He hung up.

On the other side of town, a large shaggy dog was leaving a phone booth.

Spies!

"**A**NYWAY," THOUGHT WILBY-THE-DOG as he padded onto the Coverly porch, "I've always got a bed here." A few minutes later, he was lying comfortably in Chiffon's basket. Francesca had just let him in, scolded him, and gone upstairs. The house was dark and quiet. Wilby slept.

The sound of a doorbell ringing in the middle of the night awoke him. He climbed awkwardly out of the basket and stood listening. Stephano was coming downstairs. Wilby heard him open the front door and ask, "What is it, Thurm?"

A low, familiar voice answered: "I have news of the utmost importance. I must see Dr. Andrassy at once."

Wilby heard the front door close softly, and then footsteps going quietly upstairs. He followed them, keeping his distance.

The study door was closed, but he could hear voices inside. He lay down and pressed a shaggy ear to the crack under the door. Still he could not make out the words. A moment later Stephano came out. As the door swung shut, Wilby stopped it with his paw. Stephano disappeared down the hall.

Silently Wilby slipped inside and moved to safety behind the sofa. Then he heard Andrassy come into the study from his adjoining bedroom.

"Well, what is it, Thurm?" Andrassy's voice was icy.

"I would not intrude at this hour, Doctor," said Thurm, "but I dared not risk the phone."

"Oh? Suppose you tell me what this is all about."

"I've been transferred to Section 32."

There was a pause.

"*Section 32!*" repeated Andrassy. "Excellent!"

"With luck," continued Thurm, "I should have the components we need by tomorrow night."

"Are you sure," asked Andrassy carefully, "that no one at the plant suspects you?"

"No one, Doctor. I'm quite sure of that."

"What are they up to?" Wilby wondered. "They're talking about the missile plant, I'll bet."

"When can you get the components here?" Andrassy was asking.

"Taking all necessary precautions, I would say tomorrow night by eight o'clock."

"Ah!" Andrassy spoke with a new note of satisfaction. "That means that the complete mechanism of the undersea hydrogen missile will finally be in our hands. Good work, Thurm!"

Thurm didn't answer. But Wilby's heart pumped

so loudly he was afraid the men would hear it.

"Now," continued Andrassy, his voice cold and businesslike, "we must get it out of the country! Immediately!"

Wilby was so shocked he almost woofed. "SPIES!" he thought.

"I'll make the arrangements with Stephano right away," said Andrassy, rising and going to the door. Thurm followed.

"I've got to get out of here," thought Wilby wildly. "I've got to stop them, somehow."

He slunk along behind the two men, but Andrassy caught sight of him.

"Chiffon! How the devil did *you* get in here? Up on the couch! Go on! Sit!"

Wilby had no choice; he jumped up on the couch like a good dog.

"All right, Thurm. I'll expect you tomorrow night at eight." Andrassy reached toward the door. Wilby was down in a flash, trying for a beeline exit. "Back on that couch!" ordered Andrassy.

Reluctantly, Wilby obeyed.

"Good night, Doctor," said Thurm.

"Good night," replied Andrassy. He closed the door behind Thurm, locked it, and put the key in his pocket. Turning off the light, without a glance at Wilby, he walked into his bedroom.

In the moonlight, Wilby watched Andrassy until he had closed the bedroom door. Then he leaped down and ran to the window: it was closed. The other window was tightly shut also. "I've *got* to get out of here!" he mumbled. "But how?"

Won't Anybody Listen?

THE NEXT MORNING Moochie was sitting on the porch steps reading a comic book. He turned a page and raised his eyes for the tenth time to the Coverly house. *What* could be keeping Wilby?

"*Hssst!*"

Moochie looked around. There was no one to be seen.

"Hssst! Mooch!"

Was it from the bushes? Moochie peered into them.

"That you, Wilby?" he asked as a shaggy dog emerged. "Gosh, I've been worried about you, boy." He patted the dog's head affectionately.

"Will you stop *patting* me!" said Wilby crossly.

"Where've you been?" asked Moochie.

"Locked up in that house. They've been watching me like hawks!"

"How'd you get out?" asked Moochie with interest.

"Had to slide down a laundry chute into the cellar," said Wilby, with some pride at his cleverness. Then he added excitedly, "Look, Moochie, we've got to get help! That house is full of spies!"

"*Spies?*" cried Moochie. "Swell! That'll be fun! We can play after lunch."

Wilby's voice cracked. "This isn't a game! It's for *real!*"

"Aw, Wilby . . ." said Moochie, unbelieving.

"They're stealing something from the missile plant," said Wilby earnestly. Moochie's jaw dropped. "I don't know what it is, exactly. They call it *Section 32.*"

"You kidding?" asked Moochie, his eyes wide.

"They said they were sending it out of the country tonight! Why do you think I knocked myself out trying to get out of there?"

"Wow!" exploded Moochie. "We'd better tell Pop!"

Wilby shifted uneasily.

"Think so?" he asked nervously.

"Sure!" Moochie asserted. "He'll know what to do. Leave it to me." He glanced toward the house. "You'd better keep out of sight."

Moochie went into the house, and Wilby went back into the bushes.

Mr. Daniels was in the living room, reading the morning paper.

"Pop, sir," began Moochie, "can I talk to you?"

"What is it?" asked his father without looking up.

"Can you put the paper down, please?" Moochie urged. "It's very important."

Mr. Daniels lowered the paper and looked at Moochie.

"I just found out something . . ." said Moochie, hesitating.

"Yes?"

Moochie looked squarely at his father and said very carefully, "Dr. Andrassy and those people across the street are spies. They're stealing something from the missile plant. Something called Section 32."

His father looked closely at him.

"Section 32? That's very interesting." And he raised the paper and began reading again.

Moochie's voice became desperate. "Please believe me, Pop. It's *true*. We've got to do something about it!"

"Moochie, I'm disappointed in you. I knew I had *one* woolly-headed son . . ."

"Wilby's not woolly-headed! Not the way *you* mean. He's the one that heard them talking!"

"Oh, Wilby did, did he?" said his father. "That explains everything. Now run along."

"But, Pop . . ."

"You heard me," said his father with finality, and Moochie knew there was no arguing. He went out.

"No soap," he said to the shrubbery.

Wilby emerged, shaking himself. "Guess I'll have to give Pop the shock treatment," said Wilby hoarsely. "*I'll* tell him. Er — where's the gun?"

"Safe in the hall closet," said Moochie, "and I've got the key."

Wilby swallowed hard and headed determinedly for the front door. He pawed it open and trotted into the living room. There sat his father, still deep in the morning paper. Wilby sat down near his father's chair.

"Pop?"

Mr. Daniels sighed, without looking up.

"Yes, Wilby?"

"I've got something to tell you," said Wilby. "Up to now I've been afraid to say anything about it . . ."

"Never be afraid, Wilby. I know I've been abrupt"—he turned a page — "but if I've been impatient with you, it's because you're my son. I expect more of you."

"Yessir," said Wilby, scratching a flea.

"If something is bothering you," went on his father, "always feel free to come to me. No matter what happens, I'll understand."

"Can I count on that, sir?" asked Wilby, brightening.

"You certainly can."

"Will you shake on it?"

"Certainly," said his father. He laid down his paper and extended his hand as he turned toward Wilby. Gratefully, Wilby slipped his paw into the extended hand and shook it fervently.

Mr. Daniels stared at the paw, stared into Wilby's shaggy dog's face, uttered a moan, and slipped back against his chair.

"Let's get moving," said Moochie from the doorway.

Out they dashed. The front door slammed to behind them. Mr. Daniels moaned again and fainted.

Three blocks away, Moochie and Wilby stopped running. Breathing heavily, they looked back to see if anyone was following.

"What do we do now?" asked Wilby hopelessly.

"Look!" said Moochie, pointing to a police car

parked in the middle of the next block. The boy and his dog-brother ran toward it.

Moochie peered into the open front window of the police car.

"Officer," he said, "I'd like to report some spies."

One of the officers turned down the radio and picked up a notebook.

"What's your name?" he asked.

"Moochie . . . uh . . . Montgomery Daniels."

The officer started to write, then stopped.

"Now what's this all about?"

"Spies," Moochie reminded him.

"Oh yes, and how many did you say there were? Half a dozen? A dozen? Or shall we make it *two* dozen?"

Wilby lifted his shaggy dog's head to the window.

"We're not kidding, Officer," he said angrily. "We need help!"

"Who are *you?*" asked the officer in a strange voice.

"Wilby Daniels."

The officer closed his eyes. "Wilby Daniels," he repeated. He looked at his partner in a stricken way.

"Easy, Hanson," said the other officer. "It's probably some kid dressed up in a dog suit or something."

"That's right, Officer," said Wilby quickly. "Just dressed up in a dog suit."

"It's a disguise," added Moochie eagerly. "Great for watching spies in!"

"All right, you two," said the second officer. "That's enough." He started up the motor.

"What about the spies?" cried Moochie.

"I'm afraid they'll have to keep," said Officer Hanson. "There's a landing of invaders from Mars near the power plant. Got to be getting over there." And the car roared off.

Moochie and Wilby made their way back across the neighbors' back yards.

"Two o'clock!" said Wilby as a clock struck. "Only six hours to zero. Moochie, we've got to *do* something!"

Moochie looked suddenly alarmed. He was staring behind Wilby at someone who was rapidly bearing down on them. It was Stephano. Before Moochie could think what to do, Stephano had seized Wilby by the scruff of the neck and fastened on collar and leash.

"No, you don't!" cried Moochie. "You can't take him! He's my —"

Wilby yelped to cover up the last word.

"Your what?" asked Stephano menacingly.

"My *pal*," said Moochie weakly.

Stephano snorted and dragged Wilby to the Coverly house. "Come along, you — you Chiffon!"

Francesca came into the kitchen just as Stephano was hauling the reluctant Wilby through the back door.

"What's going on here?" she asked quickly.

Stephano straightened up, looking anything but pleasant.

"He ran away again, mademoiselle."

"Chiffon! What am I going to do with you?" Francesca held Wilby's shaggy dog's head between her two soft hands, her lovely face close to his hairy one. In spite of his worries, Wilby whimpered with delight.

Stephano was saying darkly, "I assure you, mademoiselle, it will not happen again."

"I hope not," said Francesca. "I so hate to scold him. See how sorry he is, the lamb!"

Francesca gave the dog a final pat and straightened up, all dignity again. "I'm going shopping now, Stephano. Will you please see that Chiffon gets his lunch?"

"Yes, mademoiselle."

Wilby followed Francesca to the front door and tried to squeeze through after her.

"Oh no, you scamp!" said Francesca.

Wilby lay down at her feet and looked up pleadingly. But Francesca only ruffled his ears, smiled, and closed the door. Wilby listened dejectedly to her footsteps retreating down the walk.

In the kitchen Stephano was preparing a special lunch for the dog. To the usual mixture of dog food and milk, he had added four tablets from a bottle marked SEDATIVE. He stirred it with a spoon and set the bowl on the floor.

"Luncheon is served," he said with a strange smile, as Wilby walked sadly into the kitchen.

Wilby looked at the bowl a moment, then settled down to chewing it in his inexpert way. He didn't stop until the bowl was completely empty.

"Section 32"

As soon as he saw his dog-brother being dragged away, Moochie rushed into the house. He found his father still sprawled in his chair, struggling back to consciousness. Moochie shook him violently.

"Pop! Hey, Pop, this is an emergency! We gotta get moving! POP!"

His father sat up groggily, and stared glaze-eyed at his younger son.

"Moochie!" He seized the boy by the shoulders and looked him over anxiously.

"Moochie! You all right? I thought . . ."

"It wasn't me, sir. It was Wilby."

"Wilby!" Mr. Daniels ran his hand over his face. "Is . . . is it true? Did I see . . . ?"

"You sure did," said Moochie. "Wilby's a dog now."

Mr. Daniels groaned.

"No! It isn't true!"

"Yes, it is," said Moochie impatiently. "Come on, Pop!"

"Poor Wilby!" said his father. "Somehow I've failed him as a father. I blame myself for everything . . ." He realized suddenly that Moochie was propelling him toward the front door. "We going somewhere?" he asked mildly.

"Don't you remember?" cried Moochie. "We gotta get help. We gotta stop those spies!"

"Spies?" asked Mr. Daniels dimly.

"Sure. I told you about them. And Wilby tried to. Oh, *please*, Pop," Moochie cried, "don't let us down! You're the only hope we've got now!"

Something clicked in Mr. Daniels' brain.

"Spies! I remember hearing something about that — before . . ." Suddenly the shaken man seized Moochie by the arm. "Don't worry, son! It's all right! I'm in this with you now, all the way. Let's hurry!"

Together they dashed out the front door and headed for the car.

The missile plant was a large windowless building surrounded by a high fence. Mr. Daniels brought the car to a screeching stop at the front gate. He and Moochie leaped out and headed for the entrance. After a brief discussion with the guards, they were escorted through a door marked E. P. HACKETT, SECURITY AGENT.

Mr. Hackett was a pleasant, quiet man with a patient manner. He listened with growing bewilderment to the strange story that Moochie's father was telling.

"Calm down, Mr. Daniels," he said at last. "Calm

down. Let's get things straight. Now you say this information came from your son?"

"My older son," said Daniels firmly. "He was right there. Heard them talking."

"And they knew he was there?" asked Hackett.

"Certainly," said Daniels irritably.

Hackett paused, then resumed.

"Doesn't it strike you as rather odd, Mr. Daniels, that they would speak of such confidential matters in front of your son?"

"Nothing odd about it," replied Daniels. "My son happens to be a dog."

There was a short silence.

"Your son," he said carefully, "is a dog?"

"Don't get me wrong," Daniels put in hastily. "He's not a dog *all* of the time. Just part of the time."

"I *see*," said Hackett slowly. He exchanged a meaningful look with his assistant.

Daniels was annoyed.

"Look, if you don't believe me," he said, "ask my other son here. He *saw* him."

Hackett stood up.

"I don't believe that will be necessary," he said. "We'll look into the matter. Thank you for coming."

"Now wait a minute," Daniels exploded, pounding on the desk. "My son and I have come here to warn you of actual espionage, and you say, 'Thanks for coming.' What's the matter, don't you believe me?"

"Of course, of course," said Hackett soothingly.

"Then aren't you going to do something about it *now?*"

"Mr. Daniels." Hackett spoke carefully, as if humoring him. "We must proceed with caution, you know. Dr. Andrassy is a highly respected man."

"There isn't time for caution, Hackett! I tell you that this thing, whatever it is they've stolen, is being shipped out of the country *tonight* — less than four hours from now."

Hackett looked at him with carefully disguised interest.

"You have no idea, I suppose, precisely what it is that they're shipping out?"

"How would I know *precisely?*" asked Daniels, impatiently. "It's called Section 32, or something like that."

It was as though his father had pulled a high-powered switch, Moochie decided. The two men jerked upright, the polite unbelieving smiles erased from their faces.

"Section 32!" said Hackett sharply. "Are you sure?"

"That's what the dog said," replied Daniels triumphantly.

Moochie's sharp eyes saw one of Hackett's hands move under his desk. Perhaps he was pressing a buzzer, the boy thought.

"You still insist a dog told you this?" asked Hackett.

"Look, why don't you ask *him*," said Daniels, pointing to Moochie. "He's the dog's brother."

"Just now, Mr. Daniels, it's you we're interested in."

"Why me?" asked Daniels loudly. "I don't have anything to do with all this. I'm just an innocent bystander. I come here in good faith — I tell a simple straightforward story. Just because my son happens to be a dog, you — you look at me as if I had wheels in my head!"

Moochie felt they were getting somewhere at last — he didn't know *where*, though. And he was not really worried about Wilby. He looked at the clock on the wall. It was after seven o'clock! He stood up.

"Excuse me, sir. It's getting late. Mom'll be worried about us."

"I don't see any reason why you can't go, young fellow," said Hackett.

"Good!" said Daniels, getting to his feet. "I've had enough of this."

Hackett interrupted quickly. "I said the *boy* could go. I'll have to ask *you* to remain awhile longer, Mr. Daniels. Just a few more questions. Betts!" he said to his assistant, "will you send this young man home in a company car?" He nodded pleasantly to Moochie. "Good-bye, son. And thanks."

Moochie scooted out. Hackett went to the door, motioned in two men waiting outside, closed the door after them, locked it, and turned grimly to Daniels.

"Now, Mr. Daniels, we've had our little joke about the dog. Suppose we get down to facts." He looked at Mr. Daniels coldly. "I want to know just *how, when,* and *where* you found out about Section 32."

Daniels lifted a hand feebly. He opened his mouth to speak, but no sound came out.

Caught!

WILBY LAY WITHOUT MOVING in Chiffon's basket in the Coverly kitchen. He had been sleeping heavily all afternoon. The sedatives that Stephano had mixed with the dog food had done their work. Precious time was passing, and still Wilby slept on.

Finally, though, a sound did get through to his consciousness. It was Dr. Andrassy's voice, calling, "Stephano!"

Wilby fought to open his eyes, and saw a very blurred Stephano standing in the doorway. Then the effort became too much — his eyes closed. But Andrassy's voice went on:

"I've just returned from the museum; our plan is all worked out. Come upstairs — I'll go over it with you."

"Yes sir," came Stephano's voice.

Wilby tried to open his eyes again. In vain. But Andrassy's next words kept him from slipping back to sleep.

"Is my niece home?"

"No sir, not yet. She said she was going shopping."

"Good."

"I *must* stay awake," said Wilby to himself, trying as hard as he could to concentrate. "Stay awake. Important to listen."

The sound of men going upstairs brought the dog to a sitting position. Awkwardly he scrambled out of the basket and fell flat.

"Must hurry," he told himself as he struggled toward the stairs. It took tremendous effort to climb to the second floor. Time and again he stopped, panting for breath and clawing at the carpeted stairs to keep from slipping back down. But at last he reached the top.

Through the open study door he heard Andrassy saying, "This is a sketch of the packing case containing the small fossils . . ."

Mustering all his strength and determination, Wilby rose and walked through the study door, staggering a little. He made his way to the sofa, padded behind it, and dropped heavily to the floor.

"What was that?" asked Andrassy sharply.

"I don't know," answered Stephano, tensing.

Andrassy got up from the desk and started for the door. Catching sight of the dog behind the sofa, he stopped.

"Chiffon!" he said with relief and returned to the desk. He picked up the sketch again and continued his instructions to Stephano. "When Thurm arrives with the components of Section 32, take them to my office at the museum . . ."

Wilby came out from behind the sofa and sat listening intently.

"You will find the packing case containing the Etruscan fossils," continued Andrassy. "Some are genuine. Some are designed to hold the parts that Thurm is bringing us. They are shown here as *a, b, c,* and so on . . ."

Stephano was bent over the sketch.

"I understand," he said.

So intently was Wilby listening that he failed to notice his shaggy hair was disappearing. The shape-shifting had begun again!

Andrassy went on. "The packing case is to be shipped on the midnight plane. It will be picked up by a certain person from the museum in Rome."

"But suppose the authorities open the case?" asked Stephano.

"It's not likely, when such a fragile and priceless collection is being sent to such a distinguished man . . ."

Stephano seemed thunderstruck.

"You mean *Anders?*" he asked. "Anders himself?"

"Silence!" ordered Andrassy. "You have instructions never to mention his name!"

"What harm can it do? We're alone."

By now, Wilby's transformation was complete. Wearing his suit from the night before, he was sitting up on his haunches like a dog, watching the men with

an air of intense concentration. He suddenly became aware that his position was quite uncomfortable. Looking down, he caught sight of himself! His heart leaped — his throat tightened. On all fours, he started crawling behind the sofa.

The two men were upon him in an instant.

"What are *you* doing here?" asked Andrassy in a deadly voice.

"No need to ask," interrupted Stephano. "He's heard. And I can make him forget."

"No!" cried Andrassy. "Not now — not yet! Tie him up and lock him in the dressing room!"

Stephano clapped a heavy hand over Wilby's mouth and dragged him toward Andrassy's dressing room.

Escape

THE DRESSING ROOM in which Stephano had shut Wilby was small, but fortunately not completely dark. High up was a window which let in a little light. It was too small to climb through, however, even if Wilby could have climbed. And there was no chance of that. Bound hand and foot, he could not even stand without losing his balance, much less climb. His mouth was gagged so tight he could hardly breathe. All he could do was listen.

With one ear pressed against the door, he tried to follow the conversation outside. The voices were low; he could catch only a word now and then. Somewhere in the house a clock was striking.

"Eight o'clock!" he heard Andrassy say. "Thurm should be here any minute!" There was a pause; then

Andrassy said in a low but deadly voice, "I want no slip-ups."

There was the sound of a car in the driveway below. Wilby heard someone leave the study quickly, then noises downstairs . . . a door closing . . . feet coming upstairs . . . Thurm's voice.

"Doctor, we're in trouble!"

"You didn't get it?" from Andrassy.

"Yes, I have it." A pause. "Section 32, complete. But something's gone wrong at the plant."

"What do you mean?"

"There's an investigation of some kind going on. I had to answer a few troublesome questions."

"You knew the right answers, I trust?"

"Of course, but I didn't like the sound of the questions. I'm not sure I wasn't followed here."

A pause.

"We'll have to use the emergency plan," Andrassy's voice said. "What about the boat?"

"It's tied up at Walker's Dock — ready to go." That was Stephano's voice.

"Very well. Bring my car around."

"What about the boy?" from Stephano.

"We'll be out of the country before they find him," replied Andrassy.

Wilby struggled vainly with his bonds. Andrassy's and Thurm's voices rose and fell. They were talking rapidly, but too low for Wilby to make out more than snatches now and then.

". . . don't understand . . . What could have gone wrong?"

". . . can't be sure . . ."

Suddenly Wilby heard Andrassy's voice rise sharply. "Yes? What do you want?"

"I just wanted to tell you" — it was Francesca speaking! — "that I'm going out with Buzz Miller."

"I'm sorry, Francesca, but I've been called away for a few days. It's rather short notice, I know, but you must come with me."

"If you don't mind, I prefer to stay here."

"You'll do as I say!" Andrassy's voice was hard.

"I *told* you — I'm not going!" said Francesca firmly.

"Francesca, you're an intelligent girl. I don't believe I have to make needless threats." His voice was chilling. "Take her to her room, Stephano. See that she packs what she will need. *And hurry!*"

Wilby fought to free himself, but he was expertly tied. Every movement seemed to draw the bonds tighter.

On the street below, a car from the missile plant was pulling up in front of the Daniels house. Moochie stepped out, waved, and started up the walk to his house. As the car pulled out of sight, however, he turned around and tore across the street. Into the bushes beside the porch of the Coverly house he dived, just as the front door opened.

Darkness had fallen, but he could make out Andrassy, Francesca, and someone else. From the back of the house a black Ferrari was pulling out of the driveway. The three figures hustled into the car as it stopped. Andrassy spoke briefly to the driver (was it Stephano?), and Moochie could hear only part of what he said.

". . . don't want to attract attention . . . Drive at a normal speed . . ."

The black car slipped silently down the street and out of sight.

Moochie dashed up the porch steps and tried the front door of the Coverly house. It was locked.

Upstairs in the darkness, Wilby was struggling wildly. He wanted to cry out, to yell for help, but he could only snort and choke. Suddenly the bonds on wrists and ankles cut less sharply. Were they loosening? At the same instant, he experienced a familiar sensation: he was shape-shifting again! His hands and feet were turning into paws, and his dog paws would easily slip out of the cords!

"Come on, *canis!* Come on, *corpore! Canis corpore transmute! Canis corpore* — let's go!"

Downstairs, Moochie had found an open window and was climbing in.

"Wilby! Here, Wilby!" he called.

There was no answer.

Moochie wandered through the empty first floor, calling. Still calling, he mounted the stairs.

"Heeeeere, Wilby!"

In the wardrobe, Wilby heard him. One paw came free! He clawed at the gag on his mouth and ripped it off.

"Hey, Moochie! In here!"

"Where are you?" Moochie's voice was nearer.

Wilby, now completely free, scratched frantically on the door of the dressing room.

"IN HERE!"

An instant later, Moochie was unlocking the dressing room door.

"What's going on?" he asked.

"They're getting away!" yelled Wilby. "Walker's Dock! *Come on* . . . we gotta stop them!"

Out of the room he bounded and down the stairs, Moochie close behind.

In all the commotion, Wilby and Moochie had not heard Buzz drive up in his sports car. Nor did they know that he was hurrying toward the front door from the outside, just as they were racing toward it from the inside.

The door burst open as Wilby and Moochie rushed out. Wilby ducked between Buzz's legs, and with one

bound leaped down the steps. Buzz and Moochie collided head on and crashed to the porch floor.

Buzz was furious.

"Someday I'm going to murder that dog!"

As he and Moochie picked themselves up, the sound of grinding gears brought them around. Buzz's yellow sports car was picking up speed — and behind the wheel was a shaggy dog!

The Chase

"**H**EY, YOU MANGY CUR!" yelled Buzz, chasing frantically after his disappearing yellow car. "Come back with my car, you canine crook!"

"He's after the spies!" cried Moochie at his heels.

A police car was driving toward them.

"Get him! Get him!" Buzz called to the officers, pointing down the street. "That shaggy dog stole my car!"

Moochie recognized Officer Hanson. The officer looked pale but determined.

"It's no use," Hanson was saying to his companion. "I can't duck it any longer. *Follow that dog!*"

The patrol car made a screaming U-turn in the empty street.

"Wait!" yelled Buzz. "I'm coming with you!"

But the patrol car roared off, leaving Buzz and Moochie standing at the curb.

"Never mind," cried Moochie. "Here comes Pop!"

The Daniels car pulled to a stop in front of the house. Moochie and Buzz raced toward it, as Mr. Daniels, disheveled, his wilting shirt collar open, started to climb out of the car. The boys immediately pushed him back in, scrambled in beside him, and slammed the door.

"Follow that police car, Pop! Hurry!" cried Moochie.

"Montgomery," said his father hoarsely, "I . . ."

"Please, Pop! We can't let 'em get away!"

"You don't know what you're doing to me," said Mr. Daniels pitifully. "I need a rest. I've got to lie down somewhere."

"Don't worry, Pop. We'll catch those spies. Here we go!"

"Here we go . . ." repeated Mr. Daniels dazedly. He started the engine again and put the car in gear.

Fast through the night drove a black Ferrari . . . followed by a yellow sports car driven by a large shaggy dog . . . followed by Patrol Car Number 12 . . . followed by the Daniels car.

In the patrol car, Hanson picked up the radiophone and called in the following message to the station:

"Patrol Car 12. Hanson, Code 22. We are pursuing stolen car traveling west on Highway 16 at high rate of speed. Request other police units be notified."

There was no answer. Hanson began again:

"Repeat. Patrol Car 12. We are pursuing stolen car. Traveling west on Highway 16. Description of suspect as follows: large shaggy dog, dirty white, breed unknown . . ."

The receiver crackled. A voice that also crackled, demanded, "Patrol Car 12. Repeat description of suspect. Over."

Hanson looked strained, but began again: "Patrol Car 12. Hanson. Repeat description of suspect as follows: large shaggy dog, dirty white color —"

"Hanson!" spluttered the receiver. "This is the captain. What's the matter with you?"

Hanson's jaw was set. He spoke grimly: "Patrol Car 12. Hanson. We are pursuing stolen car. Suspect identified as large shaggy dog. Explain later. Hanson. Out."

And he switched off the radio.

Wilby was gaining on the Ferrari. At this rate, he thought, he might reach the dock as soon as Andrassy. He noticed that the police siren behind him seemed to be getting louder. Glancing in the rear-view mirror, he gasped, and his heart jumped a beat.

Seconds later the patrol car came abreast of the yellow sports car, forcing it to the side of the highway. Hanson and Kelly leaped out, guns drawn. Cautiously they moved in on Wilby. Hanson dragged him out by the scruff of his shaggy neck.

"No! No! Please!" cried Wilby. "They're getting away!"

"That so?" answered Hanson. "Well, I've got *you*. I'll settle for that. Now, over there . . ." and he prodded Wilby with his revolver.

Following orders, Wilby stood up on his hind legs and leaned on the car engine. Hanson systematically frisked his fur for concealed weapons.

"Hanson!" said Kelly.

"Well, it's possible, isn't it?" asked Hanson defensively.

"Officer," interrupted Wilby desperately, "we'll never catch them now. You don't know what you're doing!"

Hanson ignored the warning. "Where's your driver's license?" he asked the dog.

"Look out!" yelled Kelly.

With a snarl, Wilby twisted loose from Hanson and leaped toward the patrol car. The men had left the engine running! Scrambling behind the wheel, Wilby roared off.

Through the night sped a black Ferrari . . . followed by Patrol Car Number 12 driven by large shaggy dog . . . followed by two police officers in a yellow sports car . . . followed by the Daniels car.

Patrol Car Number 7 waited at the next intersection on Highway 16. As Patrol Car Number 12 sped by, both officers in Car 7 stared and craned their necks.

"*That* wasn't Hanson!" said the first officer.

The second one flicked on the radio telephone. "Patrol Car 7. Patrol Car 7. Mercer. Request additional instructions. Over."

"You have your instructions," came the captain's voice. "Pick up Hanson and Kelly."

"Wish to report mobile unit assigned to Hanson and Kelly passed this point a moment ago. Officers Hanson and Kelly were not in it. Over."

"Oh, really?" asked the captain in a dangerous tone. "Who *was* in it?"

"A large shaggy dog, sir. Description as follows: color, dirty white . . ."

In a poorly lighted warehouse area, Wilby was driving the patrol car down one of many crooked, narrow streets. He had lost the Ferrari. Now he was trying to find Walker's Dock. At last he rounded a turn, and there was the waterfront. Dimly he thought he could make out — yes, it was! The Ferrari was parked beside a long dock. The car was empty.

The Fight

WILBY PULLED UP BEHIND THE FERRARI and jumped out of the patrol car. At the far end of the dock floated a powerful motor cruiser, its engine throbbing.

Down the length of the dock Wilby raced. Someone was standing on the dock near the boat, casting off the stern line. Wilby made a flying leap, hit him full in the chest, and knocked him into the water. It was Thurm. Clutching wildly at a piling, Wilby barely saved himself from going over too.

Wilby turned toward the cruiser and saw that it was rapidly drifting away from the dock. Taking a moment to measure the distance, he leaped and hit the deck, skidding on all four paws.

At that moment Andrassy suddenly gunned the powerful motor. Wilby lost his footing as the cruiser leaped

to life. Slipping and sliding, Wilby-the-dog lunged toward Andrassy and grabbed him with his teeth by the coattail. Andrassy, caught off guard by the unexpected attack, lost his hold on the wheel. The wheel slewed around, and the boat turned abruptly, heading full speed for the dock.

From the bow, Stephano had caught sight of the dog — that cursed dog, Chiffon! In a fury, he grabbed a wrench and rushed toward Wilby, who was still tugging and snarling at Andrassy. But just as Stephano reached them, the unguided boat hit the side of the dock and caromed away.

The jolt knocked Andrassy, Stephano, and the dog off their feet. Andrassy struggled back to the wheel. Wilby bounded up, then pounced on the prone Stephano, and the two of them rolled about, locked in combat. In the midst of the struggle, Stephano's hand closed on the wrench again. He raised it to strike Wilby.

At the same moment the cabin door flew open. There stood Francesca with a skillet in her hand. She rushed forward, and down came the skillet on Stephano's upraised arm. He dropped the wrench with a cry of pain and turned on Francesca.

She ducked, and tried to escape him by dashing to the deck. Stephano lunged for her, and instantly felt Wilby's teeth sink into his ankle. Stephano roared with pain and fell on the floor again, on top of Wilby.

Francesca, in full flight, tripped as she reached the deck, struck her head on the railing, and fell overboard.

An Act of Heroism

WITH ONE ENORMOUS LUNGE, Wilby pulled free of Stephano, leaped to the deck, and dived overboard after the girl. Frantically he paddled around, searching for Francesca. She was nowhere to be seen.

Now a siren filled the air, as Patrol Car Number 7 braked to a screeching halt at Walker's Dock. Four officers piled out and ran down the dock in time to see the cruiser speeding across the harbor.

"Call the harbor police! Have them stop that boat!" An officer raced back to the patrol car.

At this point the Daniels car arrived, and stopped behind the line of assorted cars. Out jumped Moochie, Buzz, and Mr. Daniels.

Moochie and Buzz raced down the dock to join the

police. They were just hauling a sodden and protesting Thurm from the water.

"Did they get away?" cried Moochie. "Where's Wilby?"

Buzz, looking out across the water, saw the shaggy dog swimming with Francesca. The dog's teeth were clamped on Francesca's clothes as he pulled her motionless form toward a sandy beach.

Buzz ran back up the dock and headed for the beach. As he reached it, the dog was giving Francesca a final tug onto the wet sand. Then, completely exhausted, the dog collapsed beside her.

Buzz ran to the unconscious Francesca, lifted her, and carried her up the beach to dry sand. He rubbed her hands and brushed the wet hair from her face. Her eyelids fluttered open. She smiled shakily.

"You all right?" he asked anxiously.

"Why, it's Buzz!" said Francesca weakly.

"There, there," said Buzz. "Everything's under control."

"But how did *you* get here?" she asked. "Last I remember, Chiffon — "

"Don't worry," Buzz interrupted. "Old Buzz got here in the nick of time. That's all."

Wilby, lying exhausted at the edge of the water, lifted his shaggy head indignantly.

"But Buzz — " began Francesca.

"Now don't thank me," said Buzz hastily. "It was nothing. Nothing at all . . ."

Growling softly, Wilby was on his feet and making for Buzz.

Buzz sprang up.

"Beat it, you mutt! I've got a bone to pick with you later."

With a snarl, Wilby dove at Buzz. The two fell on the sand. Struggling, they rolled toward a row of wooden racks hung with large fish nets.

Francesca closed her eyes and lapsed into unconsciousness again.

Buzz jumped to his feet, and Wilby promptly knocked him down. They disappeared under a heaving mass of nets from which grunts, groans, snarls, and crashes filtered out from time to time.

Suddenly Buzz's voice rang out in astonishment. "Wilby!"

And from under the fish nets emerged, not Buzz and the shaggy dog, but Buzz and Wilby!

Moochie Gets His Dog

IT WAS A SUMMER MORNING, much like any other summer morning in the little town of Springfield. The air was warm and sweet-smelling, sometimes salty when the wind was from the shore. Most of the townspeople were up, but hardly anyone was out yet. The tree-lined streets were nearly empty.

In the Daniels house, Mr. and Mrs. Daniels were eating breakfast. The boys had had an early breakfast and were outside, sitting on the curb in front of the house. Buzz had joined them. A copy of the *Springfield Times* was spread across their six knees. The headlines read:

INTERNATIONAL SPY RING SMASHED HERE!

LOCAL CITIZEN FIGURES PROMINENTLY
IN ROUNDUP OF ALIEN AGENTS

Above two large pictures — of Mr. Daniels and of Chiffon — was the caption "Heroes!" Chiffon wore a medal around his neck.

"Anyway," said Wilby, "it sure was nice of Francesca to give us the dog."

"That old house is going to seem mighty empty with her gone back to Paris," added Buzz.

"What I want to know is," said Moochie, "do we *have* to call him Chiffon? I'd like to call him — "

"What?" asked Buzz.

"Well," said Moochie, "I'd like to name him after — "

"*Who?*" asked Wilby, glaring fiercely at his brother.

"Oh, I dunno," said Moochie, backing down. "I guess 'Chiffon' is all right."

A car came down the street toward them and pulled up nearby.

"Your father home?" asked one of the men as he climbed out.

"Yep," said Moochie. "This way." And he led the group to the house. Some of the men carried cameras.

"About that feature for next Sunday's paper," said one of the group, as Mr. Daniels appeared in the door.

"Oh yes," beamed Mr. Daniels. "Come in, come in."

Wilby and Buzz followed the reporters and photographers into the house. The boys stood near the living-room door, watching.

"Now Mr. Daniels," said one of the reporters, "we want a human-interest angle for this story. How your love for dogs made the whole thing possible."

"Fine!" agreed Mr. Daniels.

"If you'll just sit there on the arm of that chair," said

a photographer. "Now the dog up in the chair beside you. Good!"

"Just a minute," interrupted Mrs. Daniels. "I won't have that dog and his big dusty feet up in my chair!"

"Now, now, dear. It's all right," interposed Mr. Daniels soothingly. "Perfectly all right." He turned to the cameramen. "How about my putting my arm around the dog?"

"Good. Just like that."

Flashbulbs flashed.

"Now let's get one with the medal," said a reporter, handing the medal to Mr. Daniels. But as Mr. Daniels started to put the medal around his neck, the reporter reminded him, "The medal's for the *dog*, Mr. Daniels."

"Oh yes," said Mr. Daniels. "Sorry about that." He put it around Chiffon's neck.

"How about having your son in this one?" asked one of the men.

"Why not?" smiled Mr. Daniels. "Come on, son."

Moochie gave Wilby a poke. Wilby started forward.

"Not *you*," said a photographer. "The little one."

Moochie looked at Wilby apologetically and took a place on the other side of Chiffon. He grinned happily at his father.

"At last I've got a dog!" he said.

"What do you mean — *you've* got a dog?" beamed his father. "*We've* got a dog! Right, Wilby?"

"Right, Pop," Wilby grinned. He felt good, even though no one but Moochie knew what he'd done. Professor Plumcott was right: the spell was broken for good. That heroic-act stuff had really paid off.